KILT ME

A REAL MAN, 12

JENIKA SNOW

D1522516

COPYRIGHT

He'll show her exactly what's under his kilt.

Molly

The first time I saw Mr. McGowan, he was walking into our class wearing a kilt. Our substitute professor, he was big and brooding, masculine, and had a sexy Scottish brogue going on.

Maybe I didn't need that extra tutoring, but I sure as hell wanted it.

Alastair

I noticed Molly the moment I stepped into the classroom. She was the wee lass with the fire-colored hair, the intense green eyes, and a body that had me burning alive. I didn't want to look away from her because I knew she was mine.

Maybe there was a rule about staff not fraternizing with students. But given that I'm just the substitute professor, and that I wanted her like a fiend, I was about to cross some lines and break some rules.

1

Molly

It was a hot May day, hotter than I ever remembered it being before. My hair was sticking to the back of my neck, and I grabbed a hair tie and lifted the long, heavy locks off my nape. After tying it in a messy bun, I glanced around the room. Everyone seemed miserable.

I was tempted to just leave, to skip this class and head back to my apartment to take a cold shower, but before I could do anything, the door opened. I expected to see Mrs. Lane walk in, her big belly rounded, her expression annoyed. She was due next month, but she looked miserable every time I saw her.

But it wasn't Mrs. Lane who stepped through the door.

The air seemed to get hotter, thicker, and the room grew silent as everyone stared at the man who was like no one I had ever seen before. And I didn't mean that in the literal sense.

"Good morning, class. I'm Alastair McGowan, your substitute professor as Mrs. Lane is no' able tae be here."

He had this thick Scottish brogue going on, but then again he was wearing a kilt. *God, and does he look good wearing it.*

He set his briefcase on the desk, turned to face us, and my breath stalled. The substitute professor was over six feet tall, heavily muscled, and had this commanding persona that surrounded him.

I shifted on the seat, my dress sticking to my legs, my body heating, which had nothing to do with the fact it was hot as hell in this room. I'd been attracted to plenty of guys, but this was unlike anything I'd ever felt before.

It was a desire that was intense, consuming, and had my brain in this fog.

And the one dirty thought that kept slamming into my head, over and over again, was ... *what's under that kilt?*

———

Alastair

I saw her sitting in the back, her red hair this fiery mass atop her head. The room was stuffy, hot, and even from the distance I could see the light droplets of perspiration dotting her temples.

If I dinna have self-control, I would have gotten hard right then. Just thinking about leaning in and licking away those droplets, and tasting the saltiness of her, could have made me so fooking hard.

But control was key.

She shifted on the seat, her dress riding up her thighs. *Good God.*

I moved behind the desk and took a seat. The battle with keeping my self-control was a losing one, and I felt myself start to get hard. Fook. I cleared my throat and looked at the wee lass that would be mine.

Fook the rules. I dinna care if she was a student and I was her professor for the foreseeable future. I dinna kno' what had gotten into me, but hell, I was no' about tae let this feeling go.

I kne' what I wanted ... her.

She'll be mine.

2

Molly

The next day

I stared into the courtyard. There were students studying, others talking and laughing with each other, and even some in intimate embraces.

The sun slashed through the window, the bright light making it hard to see for a moment. I turned my back toward the glass, grabbed the book I was reading, and started up on the page again.

I was trying to focus on it, to actually learn something, seeing as that's why I was here, but my mind was a jumble of thoughts.

The sound of something dropping had me glancing at the table across from me. A stack of books had fallen to the ground, and two students were busy picking them up. No, I couldn't focus here. There was too much going on. Going to my place wasn't an option either, as I had class in an hour.

I decided to hit up the library. At least that would hopefully give me some peace, not just from the chaos around me, but also from my wandering mind.

I stood, grabbed my things, and headed toward the library. I momentarily froze when I saw a very big man in front of me who wore a kilt. My heart went into overdrive and the blood rushed through my veins, causing me to lose my breath for a moment.

He was speaking with another professor but was headed in the same direction as I was. I kept back a bit, leaning against the wall, and waited until they turned down the hall.

There was no way I should be feeling anything remotely like this for a man I didn't even know. But I couldn't help myself, couldn't even think straight since the first time I'd seen him.

I was losing my mind.

But if feeling like this means I'm crazy, I don't know if I want to be sane.

Alastair

I GRADED THE LAST PAPER, closed down my computer, and was about tae head out when I saw the fiery redhead I'd become obsessed with—in such a short time that should have made me question my sanity —sitting at one of the back tables.

Molly.

God, even her name made me hard.

The urge tae go over tae her and speak with her, let her kno' exactly how caveman I could be, how much I wanted her, rode me fiercely. But some little fooker stopped by her table, speaking with her, making her smile.

I curled my fingers intae my palms, feeling my nails prick my skin. I watched as she looked back down at her book, but the arsehole sat beside her. The guy was staring at her, clear arousal in his eyes. It was easy enough to see, because hell, I had it for her too.

As much as I wanted tae go over there and drag him away from her, I just stared at her.

She glanced up at the guy a few times, but mostly she focused on her book. The little prick sat close, and I wasn't blind tae the fact he made sure tae make contact at every opportunity. He'd press his arm against hers, lean in close so their shoulders touched.

Molly shifted tae the side, and that's when I stood, not able tae be still and watch anymore. I was too fooking jealous.

A woman like Molly—*my* woman—needed tae kno' what it was like tae have a real man touch her, make her feel good. At least that's what I kept telling myself.

When the little bastard left, I grabbed my stuff and headed over tae her. I stood at the edge of the table, looking at her, wanting to lean down, grab hold of her, and kiss her fooking senseless. I wanted tae push the books off, tell everyone tae get the fook out, and lay Molly atop the table. God, I was getting hard, so damn hard I couldn't even think straight right now.

"Greg, as much as I'm flattered about you wanting me to go to a party tonight, I have too much studying." Molly was still looking down at her book.

I didn't move, couldn't even speak because I kne' if I did, I'd say something really fooking over the top.

She exhaled. "Greg, seriously." When she glanced up, I saw the surprise on her face that it wasn't that little prick standing in front of her. "Mr. McGowan..."

She sat up straighter, her chest pressing against her shirt. I noticed she was fidgeting with her pen. She tried tae appear calm, but I could see she was nervous as hell. That turned me on like no' other.

And because I was running on pure male instinct right now, I made myself comfortable in the seat across from her. She seemed tae grow even more nervous. I was transfixed at the sight of her pulse beating right below her ear.

"Um," she said softly, looking around. "Mr. McGowan?"

"Your paper yesterday was incredible," I finally said, my voice thick, but soft so that I didn't disturb the other students. "It outshone the others." I leaned back, my cock rock-hard and no' way for me to adjust it without looking obvious.

Her cheeks turned pink, and I wondered if her whole body blushed. I couldn't help but imagine her naked, my fingers on her, my lips and mouth skimming along her flesh. God, I could have come right there just from the thoughts and images in my head.

"Thank you," she finally said and glanced down at her book. I was making her nervous, maybe even uncomfortable, but I could see she liked it. "I was actually having some trouble writing the next paper." She glanced up at me. "Maybe I could see you after class later this week? Maybe you'll have some pointers for me?"

I nearly groaned right then and there. My cock jerked, pre-cum slipping from the tip. The thing about wearing a kilt—which was part of my heritage —was I wore nothing beneath it. That made the fooker between my legs even more sensitive, made me even more aware of exactly how hard it was.

"Anytime you want to see me, I'm free." I was subbing for an indeterminate amount of time. Until I got word that the regular professor would be back, I'd be trying to spend as much time with Molly as I could.

I'd already deemed her mine, and nothing would stop me from claiming her.

3

Alastair

S everal days had passed, and although I kept things professional on the teacher/student level, I couldn't stop thinking about her. I needed her like I needed tae breathe.

It was quiet study for the last half hour of class. I stared at Molly for a second, couldn't keep my gaze off her. I wanted tae go tae her now, tae pull her in close, dismiss the class, and claim her as mine.

I curled my hands intae tight fists when she brushed her red hair over her shoulder, the long, wavy locks seeming to move sensuously, as if the inanimate object kne' how hard I was over the sight.

And then, maybe because she felt my gaze on her, Molly glanced up slowly.

Her green eyes were expressive, looking right intae me, knowing that look from her alone—so innocent, so vulnerable—made me so fooking hot I was sweating.

I kne' she had to be a decade younger than me, maybe even more than that. I dinna care. She was too innocent for me, so young, too perfect. I was a dirty bastard for wanting her the way I did, for wanting tae do filthy things tae her.

I cleared my throat, shifted on my seat, and felt the hard rod of my erection pressing against my kilt. I focused on the students, all of them oblivious to the fact their professor had a raging hard-on for one of their classmates.

I focused on my paperwork, trying tae figure out the best way tae let Molly kno' she would be mine without seeming like a prick. For the remaining time in class I sat there, my focus on my desk, my thoughts on Molly.

I tried no' tae look at her, tried no' tae even think about her. But the truth was she'd invaded my thoughts from day one.

I stared at her as she played with a strand of hair. My cock jerked. I could have been a real sick fook and reached down tae adjust myself, give my dick a nice squeeze in the process. But holding out for her was better.

She lifted her gaze tae mine again. Our eyes locked, my heart thundered, and my cock jerked violently. The eye contact was broken, and she looked back down at her book. I still watched her though, breathing out slowly, trying tae regain my composure.

And when she leaned forward, just enough that the front of her shirt gaped open, all I could do was stare at her luscious breasts. God, she was gorgeous. She wasn't just beautiful in the physical sense, but also intellectually. I'd looked over her papers, and they were transfixing, mesmerizing. She had a way with words.

My cock was rock-hard, like a lead pipe between my thighs.

I couldn't help but watch as she ran her finger along her jawline, a verra innocent act but so damn sensual all in the same breath.

I wasn't one of these horny college kids. I kne' how tae control myself, and although I had restraint, I was having a hard fooking time keeping myself in check.

Molly was focused on her book, but she shifted

on the seat and parted her legs slightly. I got a glimpse of the black panties she wore.

Bloody hell.

The bell rang, and I focused on other things aside from what I wanted tae do with her ... to her.

All the students got their things and left. I watched Molly. I lowered my gaze tae her legs as she put her things in her bag. I wanted tae part them, wanted tae not only keep her close as mine, but make her see she belonged with me.

When the last student left and the door was shut, I closed my eyes and rested my elbows on the table, breathing out roughly.

Fook, if this was my reaction tae her when I hadn't even spoken tae her, I kne' I was done for. I couldn't ignore this. I wouldn't. I dinna want to even think this was just a passing need, a strong desire to have her as mine.

I'd make her mine, because never had I felt this before.

And that's no' something I'm okay with just forgetting about.

Molly

I DIDN'T KNOW what was wrong with me. During the entire class I was focused on the man wearing the kilt, currently talking about something important, I was sure.

I should have been concentrating on the lesson, but instead I was staring at his big, muscular body. The way he spoke and his thick accent made me hot, then cold, then gave me chills.

Clearing my throat drew some attention to me, seeing as the only one speaking was the professor. He glanced at me, his eyes so blue I could see them from where I sat. This little tremor worked its way through my body.

I knew about need, about desire. I was a virgin, but that didn't mean arousal didn't course through me. It just had never thrummed through my veins in the way it was doing now.

Never had I felt this fire before, and I didn't want it to end.

But I also knew that being with a staff member of the university was severely frowned upon, perhaps even punishable. I didn't know the details and had never actually heard anything regarding a student and teacher in this university.

But even that wasn't enough to tame my libido.

Even that wasn't enough to make me stop and

think that wanting this professor, or that I could get me into a lot of trouble if I acted upon it. I didn't care about anything else than how I felt.

I listened to the lilt of his voice, the thick, deep accent of his that made me so wet. It was mesmerizing, like just the sound of it had a way of making me go higher and never letting me hit the ground.

And when our gazes locked from across the room, this burning intensified in my gut, this feeling that he knew what he wanted, and that was me.

There had to be something wrong with me. I didn't know this man. Just a short time ago I'd "met" him. He'd made me feel all kinds of things I didn't know were even possible.

But what I did understand was that I wanted him, wanted to get to know him, and I didn't much care what anyone else thought about it.

4

Alastair

The first thing I did when I got home after the library incident was take a cold shower. I was so damn hard, rock-fooking-hard. But the shower did nothing but make me want tae grab my cock and jerk off, relieving myself and the pressure in my bollocks.

Once I was dried off, I grabbed a beer, sat down, and took a long pull. The taste of hops filled my tongue, coating it, seeming tae make my desire worse. Maybe drinking wouldn't help my arousal. But right now I needed something tae try and ease the stiffness in my entire body.

I downed the rest of my beer and grabbed

another, popping the cap and taking another long swig. The cool liquid slid down my throat. I kne' nothing could happen between Molly and me ... nothing should happen between us, right?

It had been a long time since I'd been with a woman—years, in fact—and never had I felt this kind of possessiveness and need for a female. I wanted Molly like a fiend. I needed her like I needed tae breathe.

And as fast as this all seemed tae be happening, I couldn't have slowed things down if I even wanted tae.

I was so fooking hard, stiff as a lead pipe. I should have jerked off in the shower, but I kne' it wouldn't have helped. But even knowing that, I reached down and palmed myself. Of course I couldn't help but picture Molly and what I wanted tae do tae her.

Her glorious naked body on my bed—or hell, bent over a desk. Yeah, I could see her ready and willing for me, primed and soaked. I went back to picturing her on my bed, her legs spread, her pussy on display. Her fire-colored hair would spill over my pillow. She'd smell like me.

She'd watch me quietly, waiting for me to tell her what to do. We'd both want it though. And that's when I'd tell her to spread those pretty pussy lips for me.

And she'd do so instantly.

I closed my eyes and really put myself in the fantasy. I groaned as I felt pleasure shoot up my spine.

"Say you're mine, lass."

"I'm yours, Alastair." Her flesh, so pink and wet, glistened under the dim lighting. She was so fooking ready for me. Only me. Her back was arched, and her breasts were thrust forward, the tips pink, hard. They begged for my mouth, for me to taste them, run my teeth and tongue along the stiff peaks.

But I couldn't move. "Touch yourself for me, Molly lass."

She obeyed so nicely as she brought one of her hands to her mouth and rubbed her fingers along the seam of her lips. Slowly, while still watching me, she sucked on one, then two fingers, mimicking the act of giving me head. In and out she moved the digits between her full, red lips.

When she removed them, a resounding pop filled the room and caused my cock tae jerk violently. She moved her fingers down tae her pussy, and I held my breath.

I watched as she played with her clit, rubbing the bud between the digits and making these little sounds in her throat. She was beautiful, and I'd be claiming that pussy like no other had before.

A harsh groan left me when she slid her fingers down her clit, circled her pussy hole, and then shoved them deep inside. I held my breath as she pumped the digits in and out. Seconds of torturous pleasure washed through me as I watched her.

Her high moan filled the room.

I couldn't take it anymore. I all but tore off my clothes and went to her. She pulled her fingers out of her pussy and presented them to me. I greedily sucked those glistening digits intae my mouth, tasting her, getting drunk off the flavor on my tongue.

I let out a harsh sound as I came in my hand, my seed coating my fingers, my pleasure so fooking high I'd never touch the ground again. I opened my eyes, breathing out harshly, so damn needy for her even after I spent myself, that I kne' being with Molly would be better than anything I'd ever experienced.

And I was done waiting.

———

Molly

I HAD no clue what had gotten into me. All I could think about was the library, and how I'd lied and said I needed help with a paper when I really didn't. But seeing Mr. McGowan standing there, looking so damn good in that kilt, his brooding expression turning me on, had made common sense leave me.

I tapped my pen on the table, not able to focus on anything else. I heard the front door open and close, and knew Ruby, my roommate, was home. She was laughing as she came around the corner and into the kitchen. I saw she was on the phone, but it was the conversation she was having that had me sitting up straighter.

"Girl, I'm not lying. He was wearing a kilt, and although I never thought that would be hot, girl..." She started fanning herself, and then laughed. She lifted her hand when she finally saw me sitting there. "Hey, girl," she said softly to me. "Okay, well, I'll see you tomorrow," she said to whomever she was on the phone with, and hung up a second later.

I felt my face heat. For long seconds she didn't say anything as she got something out of the fridge. She sat down across from me, smiled, and I could see in her expression—and feel on my face—that she knew something was up.

"What's wrong?" she asked and took a drink straight from the orange juice container.

"Nothing," I said and looked at my papers, trying to focus, trying to appear like I was fine when I really wasn't. I glanced up when the silence stretched on. "Just guy stuff."

She looked at me as if she wanted to press, but we weren't close like that, and I knew she wouldn't.

I hoped she wouldn't, at least.

I was already on the verge of breaking some rules, university and moral, but at the moment I wasn't about to care.

At the moment all I wanted was Alastair McGowan.

5

Alastair

As the days moved on and she seemed nervous as hell in class, I had tae assume her fear of crossing lines had made her not want tae go there with me. That's the reason I assumed she didn't come tae my office.

But I wasn't about tae back off.

Time I could give her, but when it was all said and done, I was a Scot that wanted his woman.

My time filling in as professor was coming tae an end, but I wasn't going tae just walk away from Molly. I wouldn't. *I canna even think about that.*

I'd already claimed her as mine. I was going tae

show her exactly the lengths I'd go tae make that a reality.

The class left, and I packed up my belongings. I meant to call for her, tae tell her I needed tae speak with her, tae tell her she was mine. But when I glanced up, I saw she was gone. A cold hardness filled me.

I grabbed my bag and headed out. I had one focus, one purpose. I was going tae make it known Molly was mine.

The rules could go fook themselves.

I dinna care about the students and university staff I passed, or the repercussions that may or may no' happen because of what I was going tae do. I was done waiting to make my claim. Now was the time, and fook anyone or anything that stood in my way.

I pushed open the front doors tae the main campus building, momentarily blinded by the sunlight. My heart was thundering, the blood rushing through my veins like waves crashing against the shore.

And then I saw her, standing just below the stone steps. "Molly, lass," I said, but froze, the words stalling in my throat when I saw some little arsehole talking with her.

He was smiling at her, his stance telling me he

wasn't there for some friendly conversation. And then he reached out and brushed a strand of hair from her shoulder.

Possessive need and aggression slammed intae me.

That little fooker was going tae understand what it meant when I said she was mine.

————

Molly

I STEPPED AWAY FROM BRAD, a guy from my economics class. I smiled, trying to be nice, even though I didn't like the way he was inching closer to me.

"You need a ride?" Brad asked.

I shook my head.

"No thanks." I was going to walk the few blocks to my place, and although I would have taken a ride from someone I knew, this guy was not one of them.

He lifted his car keys and pointed them toward the parking lot. "You sure? I mean, you live a bit of a ways away, yeah? I can drop you off, or we can hang out for a while?"

"Thanks, but no."

"Mr. Harrison, I'm sure you have somewhere else tae be."

I felt my face heat, and my body tingled. God, that Scottish brogue did it for me. I turned to see Mr. McGowan standing there, his face fierce, his stance aggressive.

Alastair was huge, imposing, and so damn muscular. He reeked of possessiveness, and this territorial air covered him. I didn't know how I knew that, how I felt it, but it surrounded me, covered me like a second skin.

"Excuse me?" Brad said, his attitude already coming through.

Alastair stepped between Brad and me, his big body blocking out the much smaller man from my view. I had no clue what would happen, what was about to happen, but I was frozen in place, confused as hell about why this professor was acting like I was his.

"I believe Molly said no', right?"

Brad glanced at me but said nothing. Finally he shrugged. "Yeah, whatever."

He left, and I stood there, not sure what in the hell was going on. Mr. McGowan turned around and faced me, and I cocked my head back and stared at him, not sure what to say or do.

"Will you come with me?"

And I was so transfixed, so confused that all I did was nod and follow him into the school, down the hall, and back into his office.

"Shut the door, lass."

The way he said that endearment had my heart pounding harder. I closed the door and watched as he made his way back to the desk.

He faced me. "And lock it, please."

My heart thumped even harder, but I obeyed. This certainly wasn't right, not in the eyes of a lot of people, the school included, but honestly I was excited, anticipating what was about to come.

Although there were still classes going on, the day was nearing an end, and I knew it wouldn't be long before it was just some staff and custodial employees around.

"Mr. McGowan?"

"Call me Alastair, lass." He stared right at me. "Come closer."

I did as he asked, not sure if I was ready to say or do anything. Truth was I wanted to just touch him, to run my hands up his hard body, to see if he wore anything under that kilt of his.

And then I was right in front of him, his big form making me feel feminine, so small and fragile. I started breathing hard, so fast that I thought I'd pass out.

And then he surprised the hell out of me by reaching out and cupping my cheek. His hand was massive, slightly calloused, and the heat from his body went right into me.

I shook, couldn't even control myself if I'd wanted to. "Alastair..." My voice was soft, so distant that I wondered if I'd said the words out loud or thought them. "What's going on?" My heart was pounding in my throat.

He leaned in close, his warm breath on my face. My pussy was wet, my nipples hard.

"I see the way you watch me, the way you act around me." He looked down at my chest, probably seeing how fast I was breathing. "You could lie and tell me you don't want me." He tipped my head back even more. "But you and I would know it would be a lie. Isn't that right, lass?"

I couldn't control the sound that left me, so instead of trying to pretend that I didn't want this, that I didn't want him, I nodded and let my inhibitions go. I couldn't believe I was doing this, about to say this, but I didn't care anymore.

"Yes, I want you."

6

Alastair

I made a low, animal-like sound after she said those words. She parted her lips for me, and I wanted nothing more than tae take her right now. The need tae shove her pants down, pull her panties aside, and slide my cock deep into her body rode me hard. I had no doubts she was wet, hot, and so fooking tight for me.

"Say it again."

"I want you, Alastair."

I slid my gaze down to her mouth and leaned in another inch. I wasn't about tae be gentle in letting her kno' what I wanted. "I'm going tae devour you, lass," I said on a growl and watched her shiver.

"You calling me 'lass' makes me so wet."

She was receptive tae me, so ready tae take what I had tae offer.

I growled again, her words having my cock so fooking hard I could have come right then and there.

"You want me, Molly?" My voice was deep, my accent thicker because I was turned on. I cupped her cheek, tipped her head back, and stared intae her eyes. "Go on, tell me again, lass." I could have heard her say the words all day long. "You want me tae show you that you're mine?"

She licked those plump, red lips, her pupils dilating, and nodded. "Yes, I want that." She looked at my mouth now. "I want you to be my first."

My heart jackhammered in my chest, my balls drew up tightly, and my cock jerked. Her words were gasoline on the wildfire burning inside of me.

She's a virgin. My *virgin.*

I slipped my hand between her thighs, felt her heat, and kne' she was primed for me. "You want me tae claim this virgin pussy?"

She gasped and nodded.

I leaned in so our mouths were only a hairsbreadth apart. I breathed in her scent, this innocent, sweet aroma that had me itching tae own her. Sweat started tae bead on my brow. "I want you fiercely." I ran my finger over her mouth, gently pulling down her bottom lip.

"Then have me."

And at that I leaned in and claimed her mouth. It wasn't soft or gentle. It was brutal, hard, and with a desire that rivaled all others. Never had I wanted a woman the way I wanted Molly.

She moaned for me, and I moved my tongue along the seam of her lips, taking in her addictive flavor.

I wanted her naked, wanted tae see her flesh, every part of her that I'd own. I could have kissed her for hours, but instead I broke the suction of our lips, moved my mouth along her jawline to her ear, and said gently, "I am so hard for ye. I'm so fooking hard."

She made this innocent noise, one that sounded like need and desperation, and one that turned me on. I slipped my hand behind her nape, curled my fingers intae her warm flesh, and started kissing the pulse that beat rapidly beneath her ear.

I needed her so badly I could taste it. I could feel it cover me like a second skin.

I dinna give a shite that anyone could walk in.

Molly would be mine. Now.

I spun her around, shoved my papers and briefcase off the desk, and lifted her up so she was sitting on it now. Keeping my hands off her was no' an option. I had my fingers digging into her hips, had my mouth right back at her pulse point.

"I'm going tae make you feel so fooking good, Molly. When I'm done with you, there won't be a doubt in your head about how it feels tae be with a real man."

"God," she moaned.

"No, just a Scotsman, lass."

Compared to me she was a wee thing, so fragile, delicate, innocent. She made another small noise and dug her nails intae my flesh, her hands wrapped around my biceps, her emotions coming through in every touch and noise she made.

"More, lass," I said on a growl. She dug her nails in harder, and that sting of pain mixed with my desires. I breathed harder, felt my cock stiffen even further, and kne' I couldn't be slow and easy. I couldn't wait another minute.

"Fook, Molly." I growled those words, needing her now, needing tae be a fooking beast with her.

"I need this," she whispered.

Before I kne' what was happening, I had her shirt off. She got off the table, worked her pants and panties down her legs, and then went for my shirt.

Each button she removed seemed agonizingly slow, so verra hard for me tae stay in control.

And when she pushed my shirt away, her hands on my chest, her fingers moving along my tattoos, I snapped. I had her on the table, leaned back, her chest slightly arched.

I pushed her legs apart, glanced between them, and looked at the sweet virgin flesh that was revealed.

"God," she said softly, her words sweet and hitting me right in the gut.

"How badly do you want me tae touch you?"

I noticed her breathing change, growing faster, harder. "So bad."

I groaned.

I dragged my hand over her inner thighs, barely skimming the soft flesh of her pussy lips, wanting tae touch her fully, but also being a masochist and wanting the torment tae be prolonged. I continued tae run my hands over her hips, up her belly, and over her rib cage to cup her breasts.

I tweaked both of her hard nipples between my fingers. When she moaned for more, my hips seemed tae have a mind of their own, thrusting forward, my cock digging intae her sweet cunt.

I growled like this wild fooking beast.

I leaned forward again, my hands still on her breasts, tweaking her tips. I placed my mouth on her neck again, loving the slender arch, needing tae have my tongue on her, my lips marking her.

"So good." I continued to suck on her neck, dragged my tongue up the slender column of her throat, and thrust back and forth against her softness, my cock sliding through her parted pussy fold but no' penetrating her.

I forced myself tae take a step back. Her body was meant for me ... only me.

I looked down at her, at the curves that made her all woman, and stopped at her breasts. I might have already looked at them, felt them, and seen how the tips tightened for me, but hell, they were a thing of beauty.

I wrapped my hand around the nape of her neck, pulled her forward, and lowered my head to lick the curve of her throat from collarbone to ear. Shite, she tasted so damn good.

She gasped, and it was the sweetest fooking sound ever, one that I wanted tae hear over and over again.

"Tell me what you want."

"God, yes." She looked at me with wide eyes. "I need more. I want more."

I growled in approval. Oh, I'd give her more than she could ever handle.

I continued to take both of her nipples between my thumbs and forefingers and tweak them, pulling them out slightly so the pain I kne' she felt was right there at the surface. But that was my stopping point, the tightness in my rope with which I kept my control in check.

I couldn't handle it anymore, and so I dipped low and sucked a taut peak intae my mouth, sucking, licking, loving it all. The head of my cock throbbed, and I felt pre-cum dot the tip. I could have sucked on her all day long, but I needed inside of her.

I let go of her nipple with an audible pop, grabbed my cock, and stroked myself for a few seconds. Fook, my dick was so hard it ached, and my balls were drawn up tight. "I hope you're ready, because I canna stop once I've started."

I saw the way her throat worked as she swallowed. Molly was breathing heavily, and her breasts shook because of it.

"Are you ready?" I asked again. She nodded for me. I stared down at the pink, soft, wet flesh of her pussy. I started stroking myself again from root to tip. Because I was a dirty bastard, I ran my cockhead along her slit, smearing pre-cum on her folds, making her slick with it.

I could have come just from the sight of her, could have covered her with my seed, made her pussy sticky and white without even being inside of her.

"Ask me for it. Tell me you want my dick in your pussy."

She looked down at where my dick was, pressed right to her pussy hole.

And then she reached down, pulled her labia apart, and let me see the inner pink of her most intimate part.

"Be with me already. Take my virginity."

7

Molly

He was long and thick, the crown of his dick slightly wider than the shaft. I saw a clear dot of fluid at the tip, pre-cum slipping down, a testament of his need for me.

I might have been a virgin, and this might have been the most wild, reckless thing I had ever done, but God, I wanted this.

"I'm dying here." I didn't care if I was begging, pleading with this man for more. Ever since I saw him that first day in class, I knew I wanted him. I might be inexperienced when it came to sex, but I wasn't naive.

"You're so fooking pink and wet." He reached out

and gently circled my throat, his hold soft, yet promising that he had the control. God, that turned me on.

After a second he let go of me, rubbed his cock-head up and down my slit, and caused chills to race up my spine.

I heard someone coming. My heart stopped, and I glanced at the closed door, expecting someone to burst in and catch us. But when the sound started to drift down the hallway, I breathed out heavily. I didn't want anyone getting in trouble, didn't want some scandal to arise because I wanted Alastair more than anything else.

I glanced at him again, seeing as he was unaffected by almost being caught. I stared at his bicep, the muscles flexing as he jerked off, his tattoos seeming to move from the motion, as if they were alive.

"Lass, I want tae be gentle, kno' I need tae be, but fooking hell, I donna think I can."

The air left me harshly, as if I couldn't breathe, as if the life was being sucked right out of me. I felt myself grow wetter, knew that although slow and sweet would be better given this was my first time, I didn't want Alastair because he seemed gentle.

Maybe I should feel embarrassed at being on

display like this, but the way he watched me only made me feel dazed and hazy. And when I thought he'd thrust into me, just take my cherry for his own, instead he placed his hands on my inner thighs.

He pushed my legs open until my muscles screamed in protest, but I got even more aroused.

"As much as I want tae fook you, I need tae taste you first."

I shifted on the desk, my palms sweaty, my body inflamed.

"I'm going tae lick your little pussy, lap up your cream, swallow it. I'm no' going tae stop until you scream my name."

And then he had his mouth right on my pussy, licking me from entrance to clit, making me cry out and then bite my lip until I tasted blood.

Alastair had his hands framing my pussy. He used his thumbs to pull my labia apart, spreading me wider for him. He flattened his tongue and ran it up my center again. He sucked on my clit, drawing that nub into his mouth, making me squirm, making me want to scream out and let go.

"Yes," I moaned, unable to stop myself.

I felt this tightening in my back, felt it move to my hands and feet, inflame me, consume me.

"Come for me, Molly. Let me taste your release."

And then it was like something broke inside of me. I couldn't help it and didn't want to stop it. The pleasure coursed through me, stealing every part of my sanity. I felt the vibrations of his grunts on my soaked, sensitive flesh, heard his verbal pleasure filling my ears.

This euphoric sensation moved through me. Maybe I should have been quieter, remembered anyone could hear us, but I just couldn't help myself.

"God, so good, Molly."

He didn't stop until the pleasure receded and the sensitivity became too much. I started pushing at him gently, needing a moment of reprieve.

But it seemed Alastair was just getting started, because the look he gave me had every part of me lighting up.

This heat filled me, and I pushed myself up, speared my hands in his hair, and claimed his mouth this time. I tasted myself on his tongue and lips, this sweet but musky flavor that had me turned on all over again.

He thrust his tongue between my lips. I couldn't help but make this small noise in the back of my throat. He groaned, speared *his* hand in *my* hair, and pulled on the strands forcefully. I felt the hot, hard length of him between my thighs as he continued to kiss me.

His flavor was masculine, potent. He swirled his tongue around the inside of my mouth. Without breaking the kiss, he reached between us and placed the tip of his erection at the entrance of my body. Everything inside of me stilled, tensed.

"Are you ready?"

I nodded.

"Good, because once I'm in you, claiming you, there's no' going back." He stared into my eyes and then, in one swift thrust, was buried inside of me. He tunneled through my hymen, making it his.

He groaned, closed his eyes, and I saw how taut his body became. I gasped at the pain, at the sensitivity. He was huge, his balls pressing against my ass, his warm breath skating along my lips.

I felt full, so stretched it stole everything from me in the best of ways.

"Are you okay?" He smoothed his thumb along my cheek.

I nodded.

After a few moments he started moving.

Alastair thrust in and out slowly at first, letting me get accustomed to his size, his girth. He breathed hard, heavily, his strength and self-control clearly on display. Perspiration covered his face, and I watched as little droplets started making their way down his chest as well.

He leaned back slightly and looked down at where our bodies met.

"You're stretched so far around my dick, just taking me all, and loving every fooking minute of it, aren't you?"

I could only nod.

His massive chest rose and fell as he breathed, beads dotting his skin.

"You're so damn pink, so wet for me." He groaned out the last word and buried himself to the hilt in me. For a moment he did nothing but stay still, breathing heavily.

My inner muscles were clenching rhythmically around his girth, the sensation pleasurable but also uncomfortable.

He looked at me and then started pulling out slowly, almost painfully. When the tip was lodged in the opening of my body, I rose up slightly and looked down. Watching him fuck me seemed almost obscene, but I didn't want to stop.

He was so huge inside of me, my skin stretched wide around his girth. But I was wet, so damn wet my inner thighs were sticky from my arousal. Alastair started moving in and out of me harder, faster. I heard him breathing heavily, his hands on my waist, his fingers digging into my flesh.

I couldn't brace my weight up anymore. I rested back on the desk, felt the wood heat from my body, and moaned. The sound of our wet skin slapping together was so filthily good. I was going to come; I could feel it claiming me.

But before I could let go, Alastair was pulling out of me.

"What—" The words stalled in my throat as he lifted me easily, set me on the ground, and turned me around.

He palmed my ass, gripped the mounds and squeezed them in his big hands until the pain mixed with pleasure. This man would be the death of me. I looked over my shoulder at the same time he smacked my ass, the flesh jiggling, the sound of skin on skin loud. I looked at his dick, all long and hard, covered in not only my glistening arousal but also a few streaks of my virgin blood.

And then he was sliding back into me, not making me wait to feel that stretch. He stilled once inside, my breath gone, my pulse racing.

"You deserve slow, so fooking slow, lass," Alastair gritted out, still not moving.

I couldn't even speak.

And then he was pulling out and pushing back in, gentle and easy.

"More," I begged. And as if he couldn't deny me, he started picking up speed until the sound of our skin slapping together filled my ears.

"So. Damn. Good." He growled the words out. He had such a tight, painful hold on me. I loved it. "You feel how hard I am for you?"

God, yes I could.

"Watch as I fook you, as I make you mine."

I looked down the length of my body and could see his balls swinging as he fucked me. That alone had me going over the edge with pleasure.

"Give it tae me. I need it all, Molly." It was like he was speaking to himself, groaning and grunting the words in that Scottish brogue of his.

And then he was holding my hips so tightly the pain and pleasure had me gasping. Over and over he thrust in and out of me, burying himself deep inside of my body, claiming me, owning me.

He murmured harsh and guttural words, ones that had these tingles racing up my body. The discomfort of giving my virginity to him, of feeling him stretch me, shove all those thick, hard inches into me, had me crying out.

And then he grunted, shoved into me once more, and said, "You're mine."

I didn't care that he was my professor, didn't care if we weren't supposed to be doing these dirty, taboo things. I wanted his cock deep in me, wanted him wanting me, filling me up, and making me scream out for more.

His whole body was tight, tense. He filled me with his cum, bathing me in it until all I could feel was Alastair.

And that's all I wanted to feel.

8

Molly

One week later

Pretending that things between Alastair and me were nothing more than a student/teacher relationship at the university was my idea. No one needed to get in trouble because we had feelings for each other, because we couldn't even wait to get to a bedroom to have sex.

My face heated at that thought, thinking about how Alastair had pushed me back on the desk and taken my virginity.

That had only been a week ago, and I wanted more, so much more. We'd seen each other every day, gotten to know each other, and although I wanted to tell him as much, I was nervous.

The door opened, and he entered the class, his aura powerful, strong, commanding. He was a dominant man in general, and everyone knew it. I could see the guys shifting on their seats, heard them clear their throats. I saw the girls exhaling roughly, their focus trained right on Alastair.

I wanted to tell them he was mine.

For the next hour I couldn't concentrate, but Alastair seemed the total opposite. He was professional, thorough, and even though I saw him looking at me, this heat behind his eyes, he never faltered. He stayed the professor, teaching, being clinical.

After class I was slow in gathering my things. I was the last to start to leave.

"Miss Crane, can you stay after for a moment?" Alastair's voice was deep and heavy, making me tingle all over. Although this was him trying to keep things professional, I knew the heat that lay beneath. Hell, even looking at his desk made me wet and needy.

I started making my way toward him.

"Close the door, please."

An even harder shiver worked its way up my spine. Just hearing him tell me what to do, his voice erotic, his brogue thick, had me soaked instantly. Then I was right in front of him, my arousal like a living entity for me.

He rose, walked around the desk, and before I knew what was happening, he had me in an embrace. I melted into him, parting my lips and letting him plunge his tongue into my mouth.

When he moved back, I took a deep breath, not wanting this moment to end.

"Let me take you out, lass. Let me show you off and let everyone kno' you're mine."

I felt my heart beating, hard, frantic, wild. I wanted him to do more than that, but showing me off, others knowing I was his, even if this relationship was "taboo," made tingles race through me.

"I'd like that."

I felt the air leave my lungs and knew that, no matter what, this man was making me fall harder than I ever thought possible.

And I'm looking forward to having Alastair catch me before I hit the ground.

———

Molly

Later that night

ALASTAIR PULLED the car to a stop in front of my driveway. The inside of the car was hot, the scent of him filling my head, making me feel drunk. Dinner had been intimate, sweet even. We hadn't seen anyone we knew from school, but strangely we hadn't cared about that anyway.

"I had a great time." I didn't really want the night to end, but also didn't want this relationship to be about sex. Although the sex was amazing, getting to know Alastair was just as important.

"Good, because I want tae make you happy." He leaned in a little closer, and I smelled the masculine scent of his cologne. It consumed me, made me even more intoxicated.

He looked at me like he was … hungry for me, starved for everything that made me up. Suddenly I felt light-headed and out of breath.

As the seconds moved by and we held each other's gazes, I felt the air shift around us. It got hotter, thicker.

"I should probably get inside." God, my voice was so tight, my arousal coursing inside of me.

He shifted on his seat, and I wanted to look down

and see if he was aroused. Hell, I *knew* he was, but I wanted to *see* for myself.

"Fook, you're so damn pretty, lass."

I looked into his eyes. He made my skin tighten and my inner muscles clench in need. I was so wet for him.

"Thank you," I whispered.

He moved a little closer to me.

"Getting you inside is more important than doing what I really want." His voice was thick. "But it's really fooking hard tae stop myself."

He leaned in another inch, and I found myself doing the same. For a second we breathed the same air. His body was so big, so muscular, that he seemed to block out everything behind him. And his kilt, God, his kilt turned me on.

And then I heard a dog barking in the distance and that seemed to have reality slamming into me.

———

Alastair

FOOK, I wanted her, wanted tae take her right now. But as much as I needed tae make the night last, I kne' being overbearing wouldn't bode well for anyone.

This part of me—this strong, powerful side—wanted tae turn the car back on, pull out of the driveway, and take her back tae my place. She needed tae be there, needed tae be in my bed, under me, knowing she was mine.

I dinna want tae let her leave, dinna want tae let her walk away even if I kne' I'd see her again. Truth be told I wanted tae put her over my shoulder, carry her tae my place, and make her mine all night long.

And then a dog barked and broke up the moment we had. I smiled, chuckling to myself at the timing.

I got out of the car, and before I could make my way tae her side and open the door, she was out already. I smirked. My woman was definitely independent, and as much as I loved that, I wanted tae take care of her in all ways.

I walked her tae the front entrance, the light outside flickering, the life almost out of it. No, I dinna like her being here.

"Thank you for tonight. It was really great—"

I had her in my arms before she finished her sentence. I pressed her up against the side of the apartment building, no' caring if anyone saw. The sound she made was sweet, a gasp of pleasure and surprise.

"I should get inside," she said softly, no heat in her words. "Because anyone could see us." She sounded more pleasure-filled now.

I pressed my lower half tae hers, letting her feel how much I wanted her. "Do you care if anyone sees?" I cupped her cheek, then slid my hand down tae her throat. I had a loose hold on her. "You feel how much I want you, lass?" I could see her pulse beating rapidly.

She made a soft sound, and I growled low. "I want you really fucking badly, Molly."

She moaned the word "yes," then smoothed her hands over my shoulders. I heard the sound of someone gasping behind me, and looked over my shoulder tae see an older couple walking up.

The older woman scoffed, and they walked intae the building.

"You're so bad," she said on a light laugh.

I stepped back. "Yeah, but I still want you." I grinned. "I guess we've had enough excitement for one night." I pulled her in for a kiss, no' pulling away until she was breathless and clutching tae me.

"God, Alastair."

I smoothed my finger over her bottom lip,

wanting her right then and there, but knowing pushing her and acting like a fooking caveman wouldn't have her seeing that I was the man she was meant tae be with.

I'd show her for the rest of my life that this right here, her and me, was meant tae be.

And she *was* meant tae be with me. Only me.

EPILOGUE ONE

Molly

One year later

I'd never seen anything more beautiful than the Scottish countryside in front of me. Green, rolling hills, an overcast sky that had me wanting to grab a warm blanket and book, but most of all I had the man I loved beside me.

I looked over at Alastair, and although he just stood there, staring off into the distance, he seemed like he was in his element.

It was hard to believe I'd only met him a year ago. I had known what I wanted, even back then, and he was mine.

He turned and looked at me, his strawberry-blond hair cut short to his head, his face set in hard angular lines, and his cheeks and chin covered in a light scruff. I lowered my gaze down his hard, broad shoulders, along his narrow hips, and stared at his kilt. God, this man in a kilt did things to me ... hot, erotic things.

This was my Scottish man. All mine.

He pulled me in, just held me, the wind whipping around us but his body heat keeping me warm.

He'd surprised me with a trip to Scotland, to visit where he was from, his family, friends, and show me where he grew up. I felt good here, like I wasn't some stranger looking around blindly, but then again, being with Alastair made everything seem right.

He pulled me back, cupped my chin, and for long seconds just stared at me. I felt the air around us change, not because it was warming up but because something was going to happen. I could feel it wrapping around me.

"Marry me, lass."

My breath stalled.

"You already make me the happiest man in the world, but having you by my side, as mine forever, would be perfection." He smoothed a finger along the side of my face. "I donna want tae be without you."

He got down on one knee, producing the most gorgeous ring I'd ever seen, and that's when I broke down and started crying. I wasn't a child, had already graduated college and had a job in the field I'd studied.

I also had Alastair and was deliriously happy.

But this ... this went far beyond anything else. This went into the realm of having everything come full circle.

"So, Molly my lass, what do you say? Marry me?"

I wiped the tears from my eyes and nodded. "Yes, of course."

He picked me up and crushed me to his big body.

"Ah, lass, you've made me the happiest man in the world."

He squeezed me tighter, the air leaving me. I loved it though.

"I dinna kno' what living was until you came intae my life, lass."

Me either.

EPILOGUE TWO

Molly

Six months after the wedding

I was scared shitless, not sure if this would be something Alastair was ready for ... if *I* was ready for this, to be a mother. I stared at the test stick, the pink lines staring back at me like this warning—or maybe this promise of the future.

I didn't want to think negatively about this, and although I was scared, I also knew I wanted this baby.

I looked down at my wedding ring. We'd only been married six months. Would this be too much for Alastair, too soon? Just then I heard the front door open.

I stepped out of the bathroom, the stick in my hand, my mind in a daze. I saw Alastair, and he looked right at me.

"Lass?"

I could hear in his voice that he knew something was up, that he could see it on my face. He glanced down and saw the pregnancy test in my hand, and I felt the air change, shift.

God, this is it.

————

Alastair

I COULD SEE she was nervous, kne' it was because of the little stick she held. I was in front of her in the next instant.

She had tears in her eyes, and I cupped her cheeks, wanting nothing more than tae make her feel better. I pulled her close. My heart was thundering, and my palms were sweaty. "Molly, my sweet lass."

"I feel like I'm on this ledge about to fall over."

"Shhh, everything is going tae be fine." I leaned back and cupped her cheeks again, staring in her eyes, willing her tae try and be calm. "A baby?" I already kne' the answer, given her reaction, and I was trying tae keep my own excitement over the situation down. I needed tae make sure she was okay first. I dinna want her tae feel any more overwhelmed than she was.

After a second she smiled and nodded, and that's when I smiled too.

"You think this is too soon?" Her voice was soft, distant. She was so worried. That could have brought me tae my knees.

"I've known you were mine since the moment I saw you. And having you as my wife made things real, lass. They are so fooking real." I kissed the top of her head.

"A baby, Alastair. We're going to be parents." She started laughing softly, her happiness clear, but that underlying nervousness still there.

"Aye, lass. A baby." I didn't hide my own excitement anymore. I'd been waiting tae even bring up children with her, thinking it was too soon for her tae even consider it.

I picked her up in my arms, her feet barely touching the floor now. I kissed her face, no' stopping until I had marked every inch of her. I was letting her kno' without words this was very, very good.

"God, you make me so happy, Molly." I set her back down and instantly fell to my knees before her, framing her flat belly with my hands. "There will never be a day where you question my love for you, lass. Never."

She speared her hands in my hair, smiling down at me. "I never have, and I know I never will."

"I love you so fooking much. I'll show you for the rest of my life how much you mean tae me." I rose tae my feet again and pulled her in for an embrace.

"I love you, and we are going tae be some incredible parents," I said.

She started laughing, and I kne' perfection had never felt so right until I had this woman, and the baby she carried, standing in front of me.

EPILOGUE THREE

Alastair

Three years later

There was nothing more important in my life than the woman who'd said yes tae me at the altar, and the family we were creating together.

Life really had no' meaning for me without any of that, without knowing that Molly was mine, and the laughter of my daughter filling my head.

I heard the shifting of Molly beside me, and pulled her closer tae my body. She was warm and sweet smelling, her soft breath brushing along my chest. I slid my hand down tae her rounded belly, my son growing big and strong inside. I buried my face in her hair, inhaling deeply and feeling my love for her grow.

Even now my cock was hard, my need for this woman insatiable. I would take her all the time if I didn't think I was overbearing. I didn't want her sore, didn't want her thinking I was some fooking asshole because I couldn't contain myself around her.

I wanted her constantly though. Just knowing she was pregnant, glowing and healthy, our child growing strong inside of her, made me want tae keep her close.

Like some primitive animal I wanted tae mark her, to show her that she was always mine.

I wanted everyone tae see that.

I rubbed her belly back and forth, feeling our son start to move under her skin, those little jabs of life filling me with happiness. Our daughter slept just down the hall in her room, her sweet smile another reason I kne' there was nothing more precious in this world than family.

And then Molly placed her hand on mine. She slipped her fingers between mine, snuggled in closer tae my chest, and exhaled.

"Sleep, lass. I dinna mean tae wake you."

She shifted and tipped her head back tae look intae my face. "You didn't wake me."

Her sleepy smile had my cock getting harder. There was no doubt in my mind she felt the stiffness of it against her leg.

"You're insatiable," she whispered.

Three years had gone by so fast, yet they felt so far away now. Once our little girl was born, Molly had cut back on working. It had been her decision, and I supported her. I was now working as a full-time professor at the university by our home, providing for my family and making sure they dinna want for anything.

"I bet this little guy will be just like you," she said and smiled up at me again, this glint of happiness in her eyes.

"You mean he'll be wild?" I laughed softly.

"Yeah, that sounds about right." We both chuckled.

I started kissing her again, and as the seconds passed, all I thought about was this moment. I could only think about being with her. "Fook, lass, I love you so much." I cupped her cheek. "Do you kno' how much I love you?"

This woman and the children she gave me were the reason I lived.

She leaned forward and kissed me. "I know."

I saw her love for me reflected in her eyes. I smoothed my fingers over her cheeks, her skin sweet. I pushed the blanket down, exposing her belly, wanting tae kiss her there, revel in the life she created.

I ran my lips along her flesh, kissing her skin softly, smiling the whole time. "I'm the luckiest fooking bastard in the world."

She moved her fingers over my back, and I shivered at her touch.

Mine.

I gave her stomach one last kiss before looking intae her face again. I pulled her closer and just held her. Holding her like this was perfection.

"For me it'll only ever be you, lass." I leaned down to kiss her, willing tae prove tae her for the rest of my life how true those words were.

The End.

ABOUT THE AUTHOR

Want a **FREE** read? Grab your copy **HERE**

Find Jenika at:

www.JenikaSnow.com

Jenika_Snow@yahoo.com

Made in the USA
Middletown, DE
07 June 2022